One Rainy Night

One Rainy Night

by **Doris Gove**

illustrated by **Walter Lyon Krudop**

ATHENEUM 1994 NEW YORK

Maxwell Macmillan Canada
TORONTO
Maxwell Macmillan International
NEW YORK OXFORD SINGAPORE SYDNEY

Atheneum
Macmillan Publishing Company
866 Third Avenue
New York, NY 10022

Maxwell Macmillan Canada, Inc.
1200 Eglinton Avenue East
Suite 200
Don Mills, Ontario M3C 3N1

Macmillan Publishing Company is part of the Maxwell
Communication Group of Companies.

First edition
Printed in Hong Kong by South China Printing Company (1988) Ltd.
10 9 8 7 6 5 4 3 2 1
The text of this book is set in 14-point Caslon 224 Book.

Library of Congress Cataloging-in-Publication Data

Gove, Doris.
    One rainy night / by Doris Gove; illustrated by Walter Lyon
Krudop.—1st ed.
        p.   cm.
    A boy and his mother go out on a rainy night to collect animals
for a nature center that releases its specimens to the wild after
two weeks.
    ISBN 0-689-31800-6
    [1. Mothers and sons—Fiction.   2. Nature centers—Fiction.]
I. Krudop, Walter, 1966–   ill.   II. Title.
PZ7.G744On   1994
[Fic]—dc20   93-13900

FOR THOSE WHO STUDY ANIMALS WITHOUT HARMING THEM
—D.G.

TO MY FATHER
—W.L.K.

We have to let the toad go. It's been here two weeks, and Mom says that's longer than any animal should have to stay in a cage. It's such a great toad, though. It croaks when I rub its belly, and it slurps up earthworms like spaghetti.

My mom works in a nature center. She catches animals that live around here so people can see them. We live in Highlands, North Carolina, up in the Blue Ridge Mountains. There are lots of forests and lots of animals.

So the next rainy night we go on a special expedition to Horse Cove to get new animals for the nature center. We eat supper fast and collect bags and boxes, raincoats, and jars with holes in the lids. Darkness comes early, and rain drips from pine needles and oak leaves.

Dad drives because he doesn't like to get wet. Beside me on the backseat is a box with my big toad, a box turtle, and some newts, black salamanders, and garter snakes. They have all been in the nature center for a week or two. We'll let them go tonight.

We wiggle down the snaky road to Horse Cove. It's like driving down the inside of a bathtub, and the road has lots of hairpin turns to keep the cars from falling down the steepest parts. Usually there are no other cars—most people in Highlands stay home on rainy nights.

At the bottom of the snaky part the road flattens and crosses a grassy place that is, well, just like the bottom of a bathtub. It's called Horse Cove because people left horses down here during the Civil War, and the horses didn't wander away.

Mom and I get out and walk in front of the car as Dad drives slowly along Horse Cove Road. Trickles of water run down my neck, so I put my hood up. The road is shiny black beneath the headlights, and stones, leaves, sticks, and animals catch the light and look bigger than they are. Raindrops and insects dance on the road.

I run up to something and grab it before it gets away.

"Good catch," says Mom as I hold up a wet leaf.

Just beyond the leaf I see a brownish lump with shiny eyes, and I catch that. A little toad. Mom catches two more small toads, and we put them all in a bag.

Dad beeps the horn twice. We run back and jump into the car, dripping, while Dad pulls over to let a pickup truck pass. When the road is quiet and dark again, we get out.

An orange newt crosses the road, walking up on its toes and holding its tail high. I pick it up and it walks across my hand as if there's nothing strange about giant pink fingers. Mom says they don't need to hurry or hide; no animals eat newts because of their poisonous skin. For each newt we catch tonight, we can let another one go.

Mom runs ahead to the edge where the headlights meet the dark. She chases something into the roadside weeds, grabs it, and says, "Ouch."

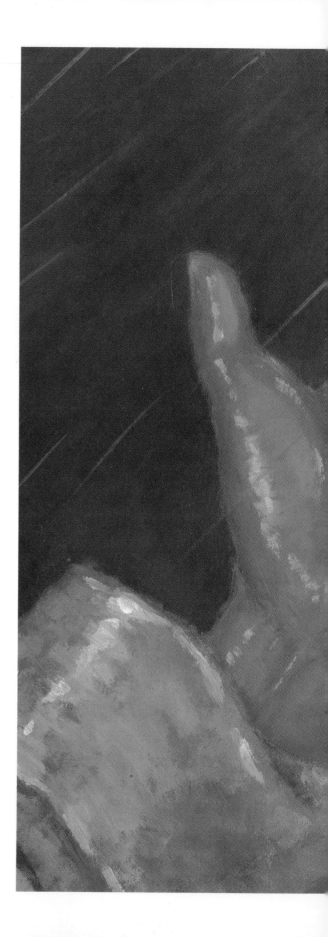

She comes back into the light holding a big water snake. It wriggles and squirms and bites her hand until she gets a good grip behind its head. It smears smelly stuff all over her raincoat sleeve with its tail.

She walks back to the car, and Dad rolls down the window a couple of inches and hands her a pillowcase.

"Big one—bigger than the one we have in the center," she says. She slides the snake into the pillowcase, ties a knot, and hands it back in through the car window. Dad gently puts the snake in its bag on the backseat and rolls up the window so he won't get wet. Mom washes her hands and sleeve in a puddle, but I can still smell the fishy snake smell when I get near her.

We start off again, Mom and me jogging and Dad creeping along in first gear. We see shiny leaves, daddy longlegs hiking with bodies high off the wet road, and grasshoppers lurching off at crazy angles. We're inside a moving bubble of light. Outside the bubble it's like black velvet. I can hear frogs singing out there.

Miniature headlights seem to be watching from the grass and leaves at the side of the road. Mom hands me a peanut butter jar. I sneak up on the biggest headlights and pop the jar over them. A hairy wolf spider climbs up the side of the jar, and I screw the screened cover on. When I carry it back to our own headlights, I see that the spider has babies on its back—lots of them. I put some leaves in the jar and hand it to Dad.

I touch the road. It is warm from the sunny day, even though it is raining now. Mom says we are disturbing the cold-blooded animals that are trying to find some leftover warmth.

Something jumps from the middle of the road. It looks bigger than a grasshopper, and it jumps higher than the car. I run after it as it disappears. Dad turns on his high beams just in time for me to see it sail off toward a ditch on the side of the road.

"Wood frog," says Mom. "I'd like to catch one tonight, but they're pretty fast."

We pick up a few black salamanders, some more toads, and an earthworm as long as my foot. Mom finds a baby box turtle about as big around as a quarter. She shows me the umbilical scar on its belly where it was attached to the yolk of its egg. Its shell is soft.

We stop Dad and hand him our plastic bags, tied or zipped. Each bag has moss and water and enough air for the animals until we get back to the nature center. Water drips down Dad's sleeve as he gets us new bags.

"We've got plenty of newts and little toads," says Mom. "But we still need a big toad, a wood frog, and an adult turtle."

So now we scoop up little toads and newts and put them on the side of the road. Maybe we'll catch them on the next rain walk.

A spot of orange seems to be moving faster than a newt, and Mom chases it. It slithers off like a fat snake, riding on the shiny layer of water. When it stops by a pile of sticks and leaves, she grabs it.

"Pseudotriton!" she shouts. She's always saying things like that. I run up to look, and she's holding a squirming fat red salamander with black spots and black lips. She slips it into a bag and it scrambles through the moss to the bottom.

The rain gets heavier and our shoes squish. My raincoat holds as much rain in as it holds out. Another wood frog bounces off like a kangaroo with Mom in pursuit. It also gets away.

"Snake," I yell as I see a curved brown stick slipping off the side of the road. I'm not allowed to catch snakes unless Mom looks at them first. She runs back and tells me to go ahead, that it's a milk snake, and we need one. I grab it just as it straightens out for a dash into the roadside weeds. It turns back and winds around my arm but doesn't try to bite.

I run back for a pillowcase, and Dad helps me unwind the snake and get it into the bag. We have to be careful not to tie the snake into the knot.

We cross a stream and watch a bunch of tiny new frogs jumping like popcorn, sparkling in the headlights.

The rain stops. Dad parks the car, turns the lights off, and gets out. We listen to the big frogs in a farm pond. An owl calls from far away: "Who cooks for you, who cooks for you." It moves closer and calls again. Trickles from the rain run along the road, and I suddenly notice that I'm cold. The sky gets a bit lighter, and we see the solid black mountains that surround Horse Cove.

On the way back we let the animals from the nature center go. Four newts set out through the grass, and I wonder if they are surprised to be back home again. A garter snake starts to dash off before its tail is even out of the bag. A little toad just sits there, and Mom pokes it to make it jump off the road. The box turtle closes its front door with a hiss.

The big toad is warm from being in the car, and its chin flap goes up and down. As I lean over to set it away from the road, it hops out of my hands and disappears into the darkness.

As we twist and turn up the snaky road, out of the bathtub, I hold the boxes in the backseat so that they won't slide around. The car heater makes steam rise from our wet clothes.

We stare at the road, but it is mostly quiet now that the rain is over. Rocks and leaves reflect the headlights; the dancing raindrops and insects are gone. Just rocks. But one looks a little different.

"Stop, Dad!" The car shakes to a stop in the middle of a hairpin turn, with the headlights shining up into the trees. I jump out and catch the brown rock. It turns out to be a beautiful toad—the biggest I've seen all summer.

Back in the car it snuggles against the warmth of my hands. I hope it likes earthworms.

At the nature center we put animals into cages or aquariums. The newts walk across beds of moss. The black salamanders crawl up the glass, and the red *Pseudotriton* salamander disappears under dirt and rocks. The baby box turtle moves in with the three small toads.

The big water snake gets another chance to bite Mom as she puts it in a tank with a screen top. The wolf spider with babies on its back settles down in the corner of an aquarium and eats a cricket.

The large turtle cage on the floor stays empty.

My milk snake gets a big wooden box with a glass front. It crawls under a piece of bark, flicking its tongue into cracks and corners.